THE STORY OF SPACE

SPACE PIONEERS

STEVE PARKER

W
FRANKLIN WATTS
LONDON•SYDNEY

First published in the UK in 2015 by Franklin Watts

Franklin Watts
338 Euston Road
London NW1 3BH

Franklin Watts Australia
Level 17/207 Kent Street
Sydney, NSW 2000

Dewey classification: 629.4'5'00922

A CIP catalogue record for this book is available from the British Library.

ISBN: 978 1 4451 4039 1

Franklin Watts is a division of Hachette Children's Books, an Hachette UK company.
www.hachette.co.uk

THE STORY OF SPACE: SPACE PIONEERS
was produced for Franklin Watts by
David West ☂ Children's Books, 6 Princeton Court, 55 Felsham Road, London SW15 1AZ

Copyright © 2014 David West Children's Books

IMAGE CREDITS:
ALL IMAGES COURTESY OF NASA EXCEPT: p5tl, Mr. Minoque; p6t, Bundesarchiv, p6m, t5c. LOUIS WEINTRAUB; p8l, Vokabre Shcherbakov; p15tl, ElChristou; p18tr, Lobanov Andrey; p25br, NASA/Bill Ingalls; p28 all, Virgin Galactic; p29tl, SpaceX, p29m, Ken Ulbrich

Printed in China

CONTENTS

05 **INTRODUCTION**

06 **ROCKETS INTO SPACE**

08 **ANIMALS IN SPACE**

10 **HUMAN SPACEFLIGHT**

12 **THE MERCURY SEVEN**

14 **ROUND AND ROUND**

16 **GEMINI**

18 **SPACEWALKING**

20 **SOYUZ**

22 **THE SPACE SHUTTLE**

24 **GREAT SHUTTLE MISSIONS**

26 **RISK FACTORS**

28 **COMMERCIAL SPACEFLIGHT**

30 **TECH FILES** AND **GLOSSARY**

32 **INDEX**

US Space Shuttle orbiters played vital roles in building the International Space Station. But the Shuttles, pioneering re-usable spaceplane designs, would prove costly in both resources and human lives.

INTRODUCTION

The dream of spaceflight has been with us since the 17th century. Johannes Kepler decoded planetary motion and Isaac Newton formulated force, motion and gravity. Another great visionary was Konstantin Tsiolkovsky, an early 20th-century schoolteacher who described practical methods for getting into space.

To achieve those dreams took two World Wars, hard-won engineering know-how and a dangerous rivalry between two great superpowers. And it took guts – the personal courage of pioneer astronauts who rode their towering rockets into the unknown.

US astronaut Alan Shepard takes a bow on the deck of rescue ship USS Lake Champlain, *5 May 1961. The first American – and second person – into space, he should have launched seven months earlier, but his Mercury capsule, pictured in the background, was not ready.*

ROCKETS INTO SPACE

The first space rockets were dreamed up by theoretical visionaries, hobbyists and the designers of weapons of war.

ROCKETEERS

Late 19th-century writers Jules Verne and HG Wells were the first to popularise the idea of spaceflight. Their works inspired many, including Konstantin Tsiolkovsky, a Russian schoolteacher with an unquenchable thirst for knowledge. In 1903 Tsiolkovsky formulated how a craft might actually leave Earth, by attaining escape velocity. He also suggested the fuels to achieve this, being liquid oxygen and liquid hydrogen.

Victorian science fantasy author Jules Verne imagined going to the Moon in a capsule fired from a giant gun.

Tsiolkovsky worked out that a rocket would need to accelerate in stages to escape Earth's gravity.

Tsiolkovsky was a theorist. It was American physicist Robert Goddard who made the first liquid-fuelled rocket. Goddard's 'Nell', launched in 1926, reached an altitude of just 13 metres (41 feet), but it proved the concept. Goddard devoted all his free time to building bigger and better rockets, but he could not get funding from the US government.

Rather than in the US, Goddard's work was noticed more in Germany, which in the 1920s was gripped by a rocket craze. The leading pioneer was Herman Oberth (centre) who published a best-selling book Ways to Spaceflight *in 1929. Oberth helped found rocket 'societies' where physicists and engineers joined to create more powerful rockets. One of Oberth's leading lights was young aristocrat Wernher von Braun (second from right).*

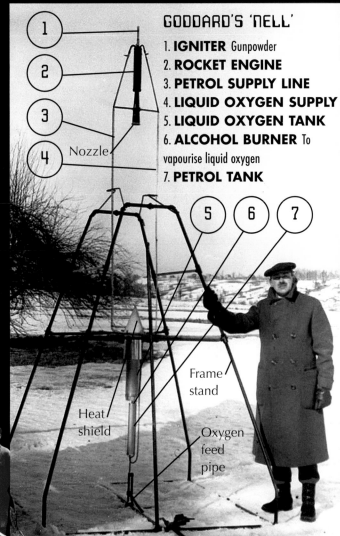

GODDARD'S 'NELL'

1. **IGNITER** Gunpowder
2. **ROCKET ENGINE**
3. **PETROL SUPPLY LINE**
4. **LIQUID OXYGEN SUPPLY**
5. **LIQUID OXYGEN TANK**
6. **ALCOHOL BURNER** To vapourise liquid oxygen
7. **PETROL TANK**

Nozzle

Frame stand

Heat shield

Oxygen feed pipe

Germany's A4 rocket – the world's first spacefaring ballistic missile – was successfully test-launched in late 1942. The A4 featured innovative chemical-fuelled turbo pumps and gyroscopic guidance systems. It was the culmination of nine years of research and development.

SUPERSONIC VENGEANCE

In 1933 the Nazis rose to power in Germany and outlawed civilian rocket societies. Rocket scientist Wernher von Braun decided to work for the military rather than give up research.

In World War Two (1939–45), missiles were not important until 1942. By then Germany's plan to take Europe had foundered.

Von Braun's A-4 missile was readied for mass production and renamed V-2 (*Vergeltungswaffe* or 'Retaliation Weapon'), but did not become useable for another two years. As Germany retreated in 1944, V-2s were unleashed on England – too late to change the war's outcome.

Up to **3,225 V-2 ROCKETS** were **launched** in **COMBAT**, **most** aimed at **MAJOR CITIES**.

In 1945, Germany was invaded from east and west. Both Americans and Russians were keen to get their hands on V-2 technology. Von Braun (seen here in a cast) and his team deliberately surrendered to the US Army who also captured their materials.

Postwar, German scientists were offered work designing missiles for the USA. As they tested captured V-2s, they began to probe the edge of space. A V-2-derived, two-stage rocket called Bumper reached 393 km (244 miles).

The USA and Soviet Union first competed in a race to design missiles for nuclear weapons. The space race did not start until the surprise launch of Soviet satellite Sputnik 1 (left) in 1957.

ANIMALS IN SPACE

The world's first sub-orbital canine astronauts were Russian dogs, Dezik and Tsygan, launched in 1951. In the early space race, animals were used to gauge space's hostility to life.

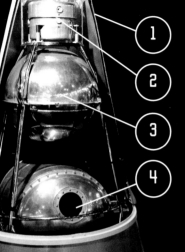

INSIDE SPUTNIK 2

1. NOSE CONE To be jettisoned

2. SCIENTIFIC INSTRUMENTS For investigating short-wave radiation

3. SPUTNIK RADIO TRANSMITTER Aerials bent to make a framework

4. LAIKA'S CABIN Complete with porthole

SPACE HOUNDS

Soviet Premier Nikita Khrushchev was keen to follow up *Sputnik 1* with another 'spectacular'. Sergei Korolev, the genius behind Sputnik's R-7 launch rocket, sketched a plan to use a back-up rocket to send the first living organism into orbit.

Dogs had long been part of Soviet testing, being calmer than monkeys. A small mongrel bitch named Laika ('Barker') was chosen. Within a month the capsule, *Sputnik 2*, was ready. On 3 November 1957, Laika blasted into orbit. But a rocket malfunction caused overheating. Laika managed just six orbits before she perished.

Soviet space dogs were fitted with pressure suits. The effects of microgravity (weightlessness) on living tissues were unknown.

Laika's cabin provided oxygen, water and food. But with no time to design an escape system, it was always destined to be a one-way trip.

10 р.
РОССИЯ
RUSSIA-2010
50 ЛЕТ
КОСМИЧЕСКОМУ ПОЛЁТУ БЕЛКИ И СТРЕЛКИ

In 1960 Belka and Strelka were the first earthlings to orbit and come home safely. They travelled for a day in Korabl-Sputnik 2 ('Ship-Satellite 2'). It was a test flight of the Vostok series of craft that would take the first human into space eight months later.

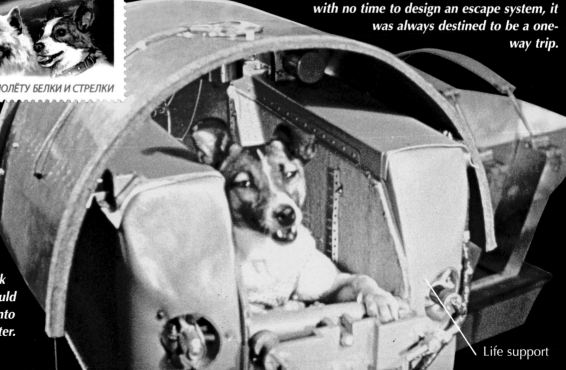

Life support

The USA's most important animal astronaut was Ham, a chimpanzee. He rode in a Mercury capsule atop a Redstone rocket on a sub-orbital proving flight on 31 January 1961.

HAM

Flight couch

When a helicopter arrived to recover Ham's capsule, it was capsized and sinking. However, when winched onto the deck of USS Donner, Ham emerged happy and unscathed.

WHERE MONKEYS BOLDLY GO...

In the US press, Laika was ridiculed as a 'Muttnik'. But American scientists had been launching mice and monkeys into space since 1949. NASA favoured monkeys because of their physical similarity to humans. The first to survive spaceflight were two monkeys, Miss Able and Miss Baker, on 28 May 1959.

NASA's goal of human flight needed to know if an astronaut could operate controls under the severe g (gravity) forces of lift-off and in the microgravity of space. Chimpanzee Ham was selected for Mercury-Redstone 2 – a fully equipped trial for the human-rated Mercury capsule. Malfunctions plagued the flight, the rocket accelerated too fast and cabin pressure dropped. Ham's ride showed that Mercury was not ready.

> **Recent ANIMALS** launched into **SPACE** were **MICE, GECKOS** and **GERBILS**, on Russia's ***Bion-M1*** capsule in **2013**.

Miss Baker, one of the USA's earliest space pioneers, holding a model of her Jupiter AM-18 launch vehicle. Miss Baker died aged 27 in 1984, having become the oldest known squirrel monkey.

HUMAN SPACEFLIGHT

Vostok
spacecraft

3rd stage

Core stage
rocket

1st stage
main rocket

1st stage
boosters (4)

*An innovative
design, the
Soviet R-7
had a main
engine surrounded by a
cluster of four boosters.
This allowed it to lift far
heavier payloads than the
US could manage.*

The Soviet Union dominated the early space race with their powerful R-7 rocket. By 1961 they were ready to launch a human into orbit.

A NEW TYPE OF CRAFT

OKB-1, the Soviet space agency, began designing and constructing space capsules. Yuri Gagarin, aged 27 years, was selected for flight from a group of six jet fighter pilots rigorously tested at cosmonaut training camp. Gagarin's craft was a pressure sphere connected to an instrument module, powered into orbit by a three-stage rocket. The entire sphere was coated with protective material that would burn away on re-entry. On 12 April 1961, *Vostok 1* soared upwards – and to a place in history.

Architect of the Soviet space effort was Sergei Korolev. Originally an aircraft designer of humble origins, he spent six years in prison under Stalin's leadership, before working on ballistic missiles.

INSIDE VOSTOK 1

1. **MAIN (DESCENT) CAPSULE**
2. **ASTRONAUT** Fastened into ejector seat
3. **INSTRUMENT MODULE** Ringed by nitrogen and oxygen gas bottles for life-support, retro engine (hidden) at rear
4. **THIRD STAGE ROCKET** Boosts Vostok into orbit before falling away

Porthole

1

2

Antenna

3

4

> *'To be the first to enter the Cosmos – could one dream of anything more?'*
> The world's first human cosmonaut, Yuri Gagarin

Gagarin, the 'little eagle' (shown preflight), was the perfect height to fit inside the rounded capsule.

INTO THE BEYOND

After 11 minutes *Vostok 1* exhausted all its stages, which fell away. The shroud had gone too and, peering out of a porthole, Gagarin radioed: 'I can see the Earth…everything is good!' Wasting no time, the Soviets announced the first man in space to the world's press. As Gagarin came round again, it was time for re-entry.

> Gagarin's **SPACEFLIGHT lasted 108 MINUTES**, enough **time** to make **ONE complete ORBIT** of **EARTH**.

ANXIOUS SECONDS

The craft spun round, fired retrorockets to brake and drop out of orbit, and detached its instrument module. Agonising minutes ticked by at Baikonur Cosmodrome in the Kazakhstan desert. At 7 km (4.5 miles) up, the escape hatch blew off the falling capsule. Gagarin's ejector seat rocketed him clear and automatically deployed his parachute.

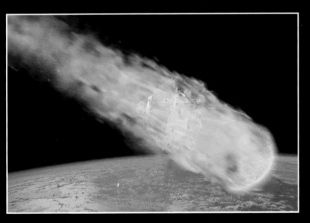

Gagarin's re-entry was anything but smooth. A cable tethered to his instrument module remained in place, causing the whole burning spacecraft to yo-yo uncontrollably. At last the cable burned through, ensuring triumph rather than tragedy.

The Soviets believed in equality of the sexes. On the three-day sixth Vostok mission, 16 June 1963, Valentina Tereshkova became the first woman in space.

Feature Index

The Huntsville Times

HUNTSVILLE, ALABAMA, WEDNESDAY, APR. 12, 1961

Man Enters Space

Soviet Officer Orbits Globe In 5-Ton Ship

Maximum Height Reached Reported As 188 Miles

'So Close, Yet So Far,' Sighs Cape

THE MERCURY SEVEN

Begun in 1959, the USA's Mercury space programme was a characteristically American endeavour – intrepid, thorough and executed on an industrial scale.

ASTRO PILOTS

Seven manned Mercury flights were planned. They began with ballistic (straight up and down) missions on existing Redstone and Jupiter rockets. More than 500 test pilot candidates were whittled down to a pool of 11 who had the 'right stuff'. From these, seven were chosen.

The Mercury spacecraft was one-third smaller than Vostok, its instruments integrated inside a cramped capsule. Like Vostok, it was intended as fully automatic. But manual controls were added when astronauts objected to being merely helpless 'passengers' in flight, especially if an emergency occurred.

The seven chosen Mercury astronauts were all ex-test pilots: three from the US Air Force, three from the Army and one from the Marines.

Mercury astronauts' training began on a 'multiple-axis space test inertia facility', or gimbal rig (left). It simulated the expected manoeuvres of spaceflight.

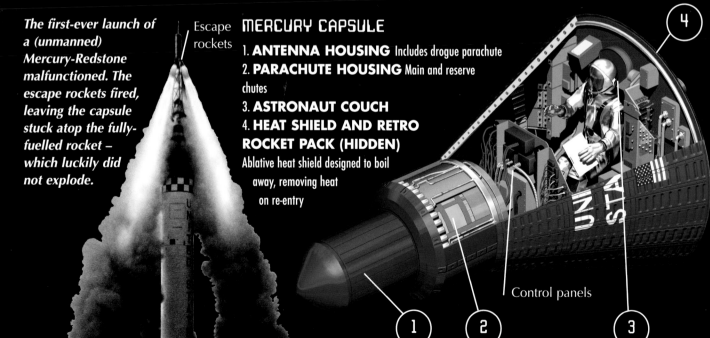

The first-ever launch of a (unmanned) Mercury-Redstone malfunctioned. The escape rockets fired, leaving the capsule stuck atop the fully-fuelled rocket – which luckily did not explode.

Escape rockets

MERCURY CAPSULE

1. **ANTENNA HOUSING** Includes drogue parachute
2. **PARACHUTE HOUSING** Main and reserve chutes
3. **ASTRONAUT COUCH**
4. **HEAT SHIELD AND RETRO ROCKET PACK (HIDDEN)** Ablative heat shield designed to boil away, removing heat on re-entry

Control panels

The first manned Mercury mission, Mercury-Redstone 3, rose from the launch pad on 5 May 1961 – just 23 days after Gagarin's historic flight.

FIRST AMERICAN IN SPACE

Alan Shepard was selected to go first, before John Glenn, Gordon Cooper, Scott Carpenter, Virgil 'Gus' Grissom, Walter Schirra and Deke Slayton. Delays kept Shepard waiting for four hours before his capsule, *Freedom 7*, finally embarked on its short 'hop' 187 km (116 miles) up and back. Weightless for five minutes, Shepard viewed Earth through a periscope and manually manoeuvred the capsule around for re-entry.

Retrorockets test-fired before the capsule descended in a fireball through the atmosphere. Just 15 minutes long, the entire mission was broadcast live on TV for maximum public impact.

At high altitude, a drogue chute expanded the main parachute for a safe landing in the sea. Shepard and Freedom 7 were then recovered by Navy helicopters.

This view of Earth was snapped by remote camera during Freedom 7's sub-orbital flight – which was watched on TV by 45 million Americans.

Shepard, who died in 1989, was a born leader. He had a reputation for being a somewhat temperamental individual.

After **years GROUNDED** with an **EAR disorder**, **SHEPARD** went on to **command** a **MOON** mission, **APOLLO 14**, in **1971**.

ROUND AND ROUND

The Mercury programme proceeded apace, with one more sub-orbital flight until the USAF's mighty Atlas rocket was ready to send a capsule into orbit.

Liberty Bell 7, the second manned Mercury capsule, sank soon after splashdown. Its astronaut, Virgil 'Gus' Grissom, was lucky to escape drowning.

DOWNS AND UPS

On 21 July 1961, Mercury-Redstone 4 blasted skywards carrying Gus Grissom sub-orbital. The mission went to plan until splashdown. Explosive bolts triggered too soon, releasing the escape hatch to flood the capsule. To add to NASA's woes, on 6 August, *Vostok 2* cosmonaut Gherman Titov orbited Earth for a whole day!

Like Redstone before it, Atlas was tested with unmanned and animal-crewed capsules first. Astronaut John Glenn followed chimp Enos as the first Mercury human crew member into orbit. Teething troubles with Atlas and the weather delayed the launch until 20 February 1962. Then *Friendship 7* was lifted 265 km (165 miles) high.

The senior personality and charismatic hero of the Mercury flights was John Glenn.

MERCURY-ATLAS ROCKET

1. **MERCURY CAPSULE**
2. **ATLAS MISSILE BODY**
3. **VERNIER ROCKETS** One each side with moveable nozzles for attitude correction
4. **BOOSTERS** One each side of a central sustainer rocket, designed to fall away

Enclosed on the gantry, Glenn entered the hatch of Friendship 7. Last-minute niggles included the hatch itself, which had a broken securing bolt.

Mercury astronaut Scott Carpenter, as John Glenn took to the skies

As Glenn soared over the Indian Ocean, he had a breathtaking view of the Sun setting behind Earth.

Retrorocket pack

An onboard movie camera recorded Glenn during every moment of his historic flight.

'I SEE FIREFLIES!'

Flying towards the rising Sun over the Pacific, Glenn reported seeing mysterious glowing particles swirling outside the capsule window. (These were later discovered to be specks of ice on the craft, warmed and dislodged by the Sun's rays.)

Glenn fired his thrusters to turn the spacecraft. But automatic yaw control (left-right movement) began to malfunction, forcing him to steady the capsule manually into the second orbit. More worryingly, a sensor indicated his heat shield and landing cushion were loose.

Mission Control advised Glenn not to jettison his retropack as normal during re-entry, to keep the vital heat shield in place. Descending after his third orbit, he was treated to an extra fireworks show as, outside, the retropack burned up.

After Friendship 7 came Aurora 7, and Sigma 7. The last Mercury mission was Faith 7 with Gordon Cooper. He completed 22 orbits on 15 May 1963.

Cooper tried out NASA's first attempt at 'space food'.

The **ATLAS rocket** has **undergone CONTINUAL development** and still **LAUNCHES** spacecraft **today**.

The success of Mercury made US president John F. Kennedy reach for the Moon. Just three weeks after the first manned flight, he announced his goal to get Americans there by the end of the decade.

GEMINI

The follow-on mission from Mercury was designed to hone astronauts' manoeuvring skills in orbit using a bigger 'twin' spacecraft – Gemini.

A 'FLYABLE' SHIP

Gemini was the first spacecraft able to change its orbital level, or altitude, in flight. It was also the first to accommodate a multiple crew.

A modular spacecraft, Gemini comprised a two-crew re-entry module (similar to a scaled-up Mercury), a retrograde module, and an equipment module housing life support, fuel, fuel cells and batteries. The retrograde and equipment modules were fitted with small thrusters for orbital control. Cockpits were laid out like aircraft flight decks, befitting the Gemini astronauts' role as space pilots.

Gemini astronauts were seated side by side with doors opening directly to space. Gemini was designed to allow Extra Vehicular Activity (EVA), or spacewalking.

In October, 1964, the Soviet Voskhod 1 *(left) took the first multiple crew into space, beating the Americans by five months. When Gemini launched, it was on the advanced Titan missile-based rocket (right).*

Gemini capsule

TITAN II

Buzz Aldrin   Jim Lovell

① ② ③

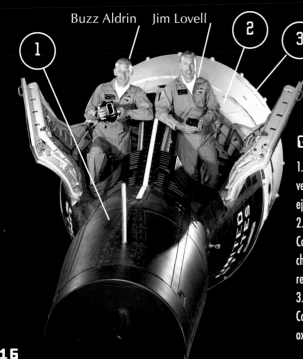

GEMINI SPACECRAFT

1. **RE-ENTRY MODULE** Larger version of Mercury capsule with pilot ejector seats and opening hatches

2. **RETROGRADE MODULE** Contains manoeuvring thrusters for changing orbits and retrorockets to trigger re-entry

3. **EQUIPMENT MODULE** Communications equipment, supplies of oxygen and power from fuel cells

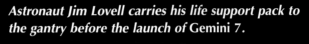

'We were just thinking about doing the job right.'
Astronaut John Young, Gemini 3

The tradition of NASA mission patches began with Gemini 5. The design by Gordon Cooper for his eight-day pioneering mission featured a Conestoga wagon.

Astronaut Jim Lovell carries his life support pack to the gantry before the launch of Gemini 7.

RENDEZVOUS IN SPACE

The Gemini missions were crewed by a mixture of Mercury veterans and inexperienced astronauts. But precision orbital manoeuvres did not begin properly until *Gemini 5*'s marathon eight-day science-based mission.

GEMINI 7

On 15 December 1965, the first rendezvous manoeuvre of manned spacecraft took place. *Gemini 6A* boosted up to the orbit of *Gemini 7* and drifted to less than 30 cm (one foot) away. The astronauts exchanged written messages through the windows.

After re-entry, Gemini capsules splashed down, like their Mercury predecessors. Gemini 3 pilot Gus Grissom wanted to name his craft Titanic. He was overruled so he named it 'Molly Brown' (who survived the Titanic tragedy) instead.

Gemini 6's original mission had been to dock with an unmanned Agena Target Vehicle (ATV). When the ATV exploded on lift-off, Frank Borman and Jim Lovell of Gemini 7 suggested the Gemini 6 crew rendezvous with their own mission instead. The renamed Gemini 6A was crewed by Walter Schirra and Thomas Stafford.

GEMINI 6A

Docking sight ————

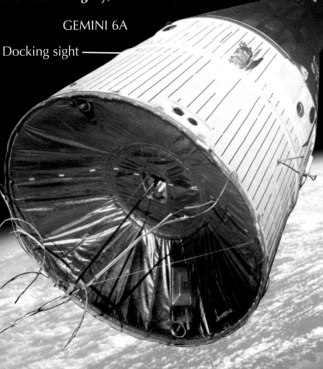

GEMINIs **8** to **12** undertook **increasingly AMBITIOUS** docking **MANOEUVRES** to **prepare** for the Apollo **MOON SHOTS**.

17

SPACEWALKING

18-III 65
BOCXOД-2

T he success of Gemini rattled the Soviets. To keep ahead in the space race, they adapted Vostok capsules as Voskhods, for multiple crews – and to send a man out of the craft, to 'walk' alone in space.

The Soviets developed an EVA suit by adding an extra layer to their standard flight suit. The Berkut *('Golden Eagle') suit had a life support pack on the back with 45 minutes of oxygen. Heat, moisture and waste gas were vented into space by a relief valve.*

VOSKHOD 2

1. **COSMONAUT**
2. **VOLGA AIRLOCK**
3. **SPARE RETROROCKETS**
4. **COMPRESSED AIR BOTTLES**
5. **INSTRUMENT MODULE**

Main retrorockets

A STICKY MOMENT

Voskhod 1 crammed three men into a Vostok sphere. *Voskhod 2* had an inflatable fabric airlock for the EVA (Extra Vehicular Activity) or spacewalk. Pavel Belyayev commanded and Alexey Leonov prepared for EVA. They launched on 18 March 1965. On the second orbit, Leonov pressurised his suit and climbed into the airlock, soon emerging to float on a 5-metre (16-feet) tether.

Leonov soon had difficulties moving. His suit heated and ballooned at the joints. Unable to pull himself back in feet-first, he tried head-first but got stuck. In a snap decision he opened his suit's relief valve to deflate – at the risking of boiling his blood. At last he bent his legs inside and sealed the airlock, exhausted but very relieved.

Leonov was celebrated as a superhero in his mother country.

Leonov's intrepid spacewalk lasted 10 minutes and was filmed by a movie camera fixed to the airlock.

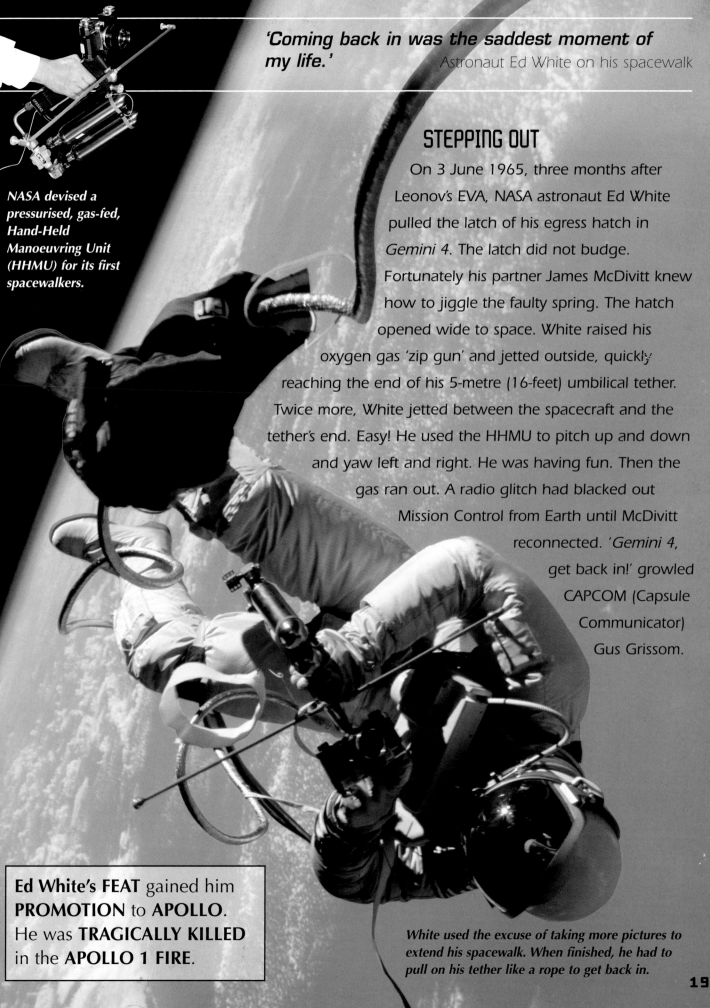

'Coming back in was the saddest moment of my life.'
Astronaut Ed White on his spacewalk

NASA devised a pressurised, gas-fed, Hand-Held Manoeuvring Unit (HHMU) for its first spacewalkers.

STEPPING OUT

On 3 June 1965, three months after Leonov's EVA, NASA astronaut Ed White pulled the latch of his egress hatch in *Gemini 4*. The latch did not budge. Fortunately his partner James McDivitt knew how to jiggle the faulty spring. The hatch opened wide to space. White raised his oxygen gas 'zip gun' and jetted outside, quickly reaching the end of his 5-metre (16-feet) umbilical tether. Twice more, White jetted between the spacecraft and the tether's end. Easy! He used the HHMU to pitch up and down and yaw left and right. He was having fun. Then the gas ran out. A radio glitch had blacked out Mission Control from Earth until McDivitt reconnected. '*Gemini 4*, get back in!' growled CAPCOM (Capsule Communicator) Gus Grissom.

Ed White's **FEAT** gained him **PROMOTION** to **APOLLO**. He was **TRAGICALLY KILLED** in the **APOLLO 1 FIRE**.

White used the excuse of taking more pictures to extend his spacewalk. When finished, he had to pull on his tether like a rope to get back in.

SOYUZ

Soyuz was originally designed as a Moon ferry. But as the Soviet Moon effort fell apart, Soyuz became Russia's premier general-purpose spacecraft.

The Soyuz launcher was based on the tried and tested R-7. The core stage housed a more powerful engine to lift the heavier craft.

UNITY

Sergei Korolev conceived Soyuz ('Union') as a pioneering docking spacecraft. But fatality on the *Soyuz 1* test flight (and on US *Apollo 1*) prompted caution. On 30 October 1967, two unmanned Soyuz, *Kosmos 186* and *Kosmos 188*, made the first automated space docking.

The pioneering human mission came on 16 January 1969, when *Soyuz 4* joined with *Soyuz 5* at 219 km (136 miles) up. With no connecting tunnel as yet, the two transferring cosmonauts of *Soyuz 5* donned spacesuits and floated across. The first ever manned spacecraft docking was completed – nearly two months before the USA.

Soyuz spacecraft have no windows for a forward view. They use a periscope viewfinder and radar rangefinding to line up for docking.

Boris Volynov, in Soyuz 5, endured a scary re-entry that nearly burned through his escape hatch. Then his capsule failed to fire retrorockets. The hard landing broke his teeth!

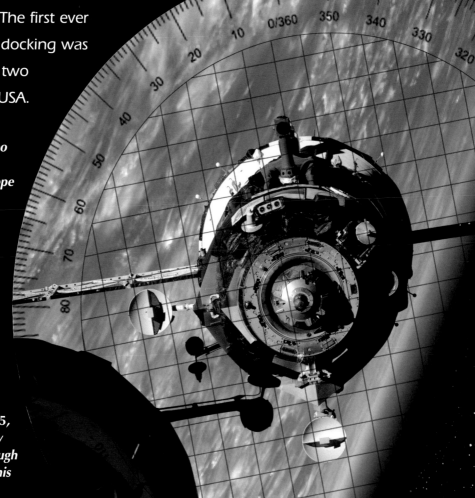

HANDSHAKE IN SPACE

By 1972, Cold War tensions between the Soviet Union and the USA had eased enough for a first joint space mission. An Apollo spacecraft crewed by Thomas Stafford, Vance Brand and Deke Slayton would dock with a Soyuz 7K-TM flown by Alexey Leonov and Valery Kubasov.

The political goodwill mission took three years to organise. Critical was a docking module that married the different-sized mechanisms and atmospheres of the spacecraft. The crews also took language lessons and familiarised with each other's technology. On 17 July 1975, East and West successfully came together. They blazed a trail for the multinational space missions of today.

Manoeuvring thrusters

① ②

The last-ever Apollo journey was during the Apollo-Soyuz Test Mission (ASTP).

APOLLO-SOYUZ

1. **APOLLO SERVICE MODULE**
2. **APOLLO COMMAND MODULE** Also the descent capsule
3. **DOCKING MODULE** With custom-made connecting mechanism
4. **SOYUZ ORBITAL MODULE** Storage and laboratory facilities
5. **SOYUZ DESCENT MODULE**
6. **SOYUZ SERVICE MODULE**

③

④

Porthole

⑤

⑥

Veteran cosmonaut Alexey Leonov greeted US's Thomas Stafford at the docking module threshold.

Manoeuvring thrusters

Solar array

SOYUZ craft still **operate TODAY**. **PROGRESS**, a fully **AUTOMATED** Soyuz spacecraft, **FERRIES supplies** to the **INTERNATIONAL SPACE STATION**.

THE SPACE SHUTTLE

With the Moon race won, NASA returned to its longstanding dream. It planned a fleet of cheap, reusable spaceplanes to carry parts into orbit for a space station.

The final Shuttle plane ended up much bigger than planned, to carry military payloads that helped to offset the cost of the project.

Liquid oxygen   Liquid hydrogen

SPACE SHUTTLE

1. **ORBITER MAIN ENGINES**
2. **ORBITER PAYLOAD BAY**
3. **CREW COMPARTMENT**
4. **MAIN FUEL TANK** Liquid oxygen and hydrogen, disposable
5. **BOOSTER ROCKET** Solid fuel, collected and reused

On 12 April 1981 – 20 years after Gagarin's historic flight – orbiter Columbia lifted off on STS-1 with an empty payload bay and a crew of only two.

SPACE TRANSPORT ONE

The Space Transportation System (STS) featured a Shuttle orbiter riding a huge external fuel tank (ET), with twin detachable-recoverable Solid Rocket Boosters (SRBs) to help lift-off.

At mission's end the orbiter flipped over and fired retroengines before rolling back to re-enter. Special ceramic tiles protected the underside from re-entry heat, enabling a glide in for landing. After re-conditioning, it was ready again. The first four orbiters in space were Columbia, Challenger, Discovery and Atlantis.

The **INAUGURAL** **launch** of the **SHUTTLE** was **also** the **FIRST** time **all** of its **SYSTEMS** were tested **TOGETHER.**

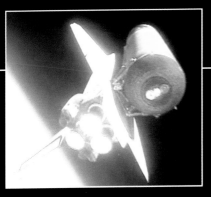

The camera on a falling booster rocket shows how the orbiter flies inverted beneath the ET. With the tank gone, basic orbital flight is inverted – looking down on Earth.

ORBITER SYSTEMS

1. **MANIPULATOR ARM**
2. **BAY DOOR RADIATORS**
3. **OMS POD** Orbital Manoeuvring System
– liquid-fuelled main rocket and Reaction Control System (RCS) thrusters
4. **RCS NOZZLES**

① ② ③ ④

Window onto payload bay

Main manoeuvring rocket

Main engines

'17,500 miles an hour in eight and a half minutes – mind-boggling...'
Bob Crippen, STS-1 astronaut

'**17,500 miles an hour in eight and a half minutes – mind-boggling...**'
Bob Crippen, STS-1 astronaut

ORBITER ASCENDANT

STS-1 was the culmination of seven years' development and testing. Even now, the Shuttle remains the most technologically complex machine ever built. At 46 km (28 miles) up, the spent SRBs fell away to drift into the sea by parachute. The orbiter's three powerful R25 engines – the first and only reusable rocket engines so far – continued to power the craft to 113 km (70 miles). Here the empty tank separated to fall and burn up in Earth's atmosphere. Now in spacecraft mode, the orbiter opened its two bay doors with their radiators that cool the ship. Young and Crippen spent the next two and a half days (37 orbits), at 306 km (190 miles) up, checking all the systems.

Veteran astronaut John Young led STS-1. He had flown Gemini and been to the Moon.

Here STS-1 astronaut Crippen floats above Earth, seen through the cabin roof. The remote manipulator arm controls are at his left.

STS-1 arrived home safely at Edwards Air Force Base, California – the first-ever wheeled spacecraft landing.

Originally **budgeted** at **$200 MILLION, over** the **SHUTTLE'S LIFETIME** the **average COST** per **launch** was **$1,350 MILLION.**

GREAT SHUTTLE MISSIONS

The Shuttle remained in use for double its intended lifespan. Over 135 missions, it hauled freight and hosted landmark in-orbit construction and repairs.

STS-9 launched Spacelab, a microgravity habitation and experiment pod housed in the orbiter bay. Spacelab was used on 25 missions.

SPACE UTILITY

The Shuttle Remote Manipulator System (SRMS), or Canadarm, was carried on 50 shuttle missions. On 6 April 1984, *Challenger* took off on the first in-orbit repair mission to fix NASA's *SolarMax* satellite, using Canadarm to grapple the satellite. Shuttles also carried into orbit three of NASA's Great Observatories, beginning with the Hubble Space Telescope in 1990. Hubble was serviced by Shuttles five times, replacing cameras, instruments, solar panels, and gyroscopes.

On STS-7 in 1983, Sally Ride became the first American woman into space. Shuttle flights opened up space beyond test pilots to include scientists and engineers.

The **experience** of **SPACELAB** was **INVALUABLE** to the **designers** of the **ISS**.

In 1984 on STS-41B, Bruce McCandless performed the first untethered spacewalk using a gas-propelled backpack.

CANADARM

Payload bay

STS-61, the first Hubble servicing mission, turned into an epic 11-day operation. New instruments were fitted to correct a flaw in the telescope's main mirror. Here Story Musgrave rides Canadarm towards Hubble.

> ### 'The Space Shuttle marks our entrance into a new era.'
> US president Ronald Reagan, 1982

On mission STS-71, 27 June 1995, Atlantis rose towards the Russian space station Mir. It carried a docking pod to attach to Mir's Kristall module. It was NASA's 100th manned space mission.

Spacelab module

Orbiter Docking System (ODS)

On 29 October 1998, for STS-95, 77-year-old John Glenn returned to space after 36 years, as the oldest astronaut in history.

HEAVY LIFTING

Finally, on 4 December 1998, the Shuttle began to fulfill its original purpose of putting together an orbiting space station. The first International Space Station (ISS) mission was flown by *Endeavor*, a new Shuttle built from spare parts to replace the lost *Challenger*. It took 13 years and over 35 more Shuttle visits to finish the ISS. Internationally constructed modules, trusses and solar arrays were hauled up 370 km (229 miles). *Endeavor* carried the last permanent US pieces of the station on STS-134, on 16 May 2011.

> ## DISCOVERY, the HARDEST WORKING shuttle, accumulated 365 DAYS in SPACE.

STS-88 saw the beginning of the ISS. With US connecting module Unity positioned in the bay, astronauts on Endeavor used Canadarm to pull Russian cargo module Zarya slowly towards it.

ZARYA

UNITY

The last-ever Shuttle mission, STS-135, was flown by Atlantis on 8 July 2011. It carried a Raffaello module full of supplies. Thirteen days later the last of the world's heaviest gliders came in hard and fast for the final time at John F Kennedy Space Center.

On STS-128, in 2009, Discovery brought the Multi-Purpose Logistics Module (MPLM) Leonardo to the ISS. It was a large pressurised container for taking materials to and from the station.

RISK FACTORS

R iding hypersonic rockets into space, astronauts must trust in complex, highly-engineered machines to transport them safely. On the rare occasions these machines fail, the results can be catastrophic.

STS-51-L, the 25th Shuttle mission, took off with a NASA communications satellite in its payload bay.

BAD PRACTICE

In 1967, *Soyuz 1* was rushed to launch before it was ready. The heat shield had been made heavier and the parachute larger, but the chute holder was left unchanged. The chute was hammered in so tightly it failed to unfurl. Vladimir Komarov was the first space fatality.

A similar mix of manufacturing defect and bad practice doomed Space Shuttle *Challenger* on STS-51-L. On 28 January 1986, the sub zero temperatures had made an O-ring seal on a joint in the right hand SRB too brittle. Fifty-eight seconds into launch, burning gas jetted out of the joint, causing a chain reaction that destroyed the Shuttle. The reliability of the O-rings had already been questioned by engineers – but their concerns had not been passed to safety managers.

Cosmonaut Vladimir Komarov became the first person killed in spaceflight when the parachute failed on his descending Soyuz 1 *capsule, 1967.*

STS-51-L crew member Christa McAuliffe waved to onlookers as the crew began their mission.

A blowtorch of flame (circled) burned through the SRB support strut. Seconds later the strut failed, allowing the SRB to strike the external fuel tank and ignite it.

STS-51-L's fuel tank exploded 73 seconds into the flight, causing the orbiter to disintegrate in an instant. The crew capsule (circled) was blasted away in one piece but hit the ocean seconds later, killing all on board.

'...reality must take precedence over public relations, for Nature cannot be fooled.'

Richard Feynman, Challenger Inquiry

Three cosmonauts died on re-entry in Soyuz 11, *1971, when their capsule depressurised.*

Commander Rick Husband and pilot William McCool were on Columbia's *flight deck just before the accident.*

FATAL DAMAGE

The enquiry into *Challenger* grounded the Shuttle fleet for 32 months. Turnaround time for the fleet was increased. The Shuttle's promise of cheap, regular access to orbit was gone.

On 16 January 2003, Shuttle *Columbia* rose to begin a mission with the new SpaceHab module. As it lifted, vibration tore a piece of foam ramp loose from the fuel tank and struck the orbiter's left wing. As the mission unfolded in space, flight engineers debated. Was the craft fatally damaged? Probably not. When *Columbia* re-entered, hot gases entered a hole in the wing, causing it to fail. *Columbia* tumbled over and broke apart, depressurising the crew cabin.

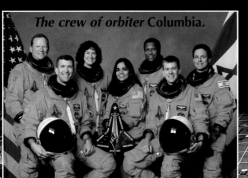

The crew of orbiter Columbia.

Columbia *broke up with the loss of all seven crew. Fragments of the spacecraft were pieced together for the enquiry (below) – and the Shuttle's retirement began.*

HUMAN spaceflight has a **FATALITY RATE** of **roughly 4%** – the **SAME** as **climbing MOUNT EVEREST**.

COMMERCIAL SPACEFLIGHT

SpaceShipOne, *the first private spacecraft, used pivoting wings to act like airbrakes, slowing its descent.*

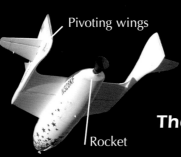

Pivoting wings

Rocket

O n 21 June 2004, test pilot Mike Melvill flicked the rocket switch on *SpaceShipOne* and screamed to 100 km (62 miles) – the start of space. The era of private spaceflight had arrived.

SUB-ORBITAL

SpaceShipOne entered space twice more to win the Ansari X-Prize. During each flight, the pilot experienced three and a half minutes of microgravity. The craft was designed by Burt Rutan, an American aeroengineer who also designed the follow-up, *SpaceShipTwo.*

Rutan's innovations included a hybrid solid/liquid rocket and 'piggy-backing' the spacecraft to its launch altitude beneath a jet carrier plane 'mothership'.

SPACESHIPTWO

1. **WHITE KNIGHT TWO**
Twin-fuselage turbofan carrier craft
2. **TURBOFAN ENGINES**
3. **SPACESHIPTWO**
4. **HYBRID ROCKET**

SpaceShipTwo *here test-fires its rocket engine in 2013.*

This artist's impression shows the completed Mojave Air & Space Port in California. Virgin Galactic plans to operate a fleet of five SpaceShipTwo craft.

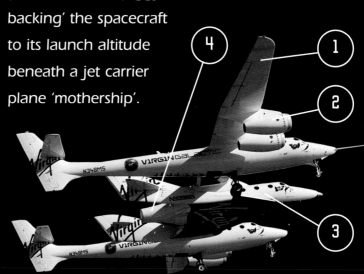

The **COST** of a **PRIVATE SUB-ORBITAL flight** is **EXPECTED** to **be** about $250,000 per **PASSENGER.**

> *'Space will probably be more responsible for changing the world than anything else.'* Elon Musk, founder of SpaceX

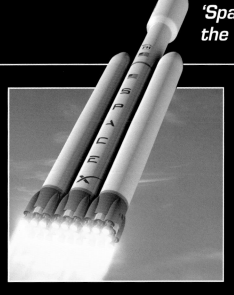

The SpaceX Falcon Heavy *is the largest planned commercial heavy-lift rocket. It will raise payloads just under half the size of the retired monster Saturn V, of Apollo fame.*

Telecoms mogul Anousheh Ansari was the fourth civilian to pay for a space trip.

SPACE TOURISM

Since 2001, several private individuals have travelled to the ISS aboard Russian Soyuz spacecraft. Space tourism does not come cheap. It involves six months' full astronaut training at Cosmonaut Training Center, Star City, in Russia. The average stay is 10 days, during which the visitor does experiments and takes part in crew activities – perhaps a spacewalk. What is next for the brave pioneers of space travel?

SERVICING THE ISS

Commercial robotic capsules are already being used to resupply the ISS. NASA has awarded funding to three private companies to develop crew vehicles: SpaceX with the Dragon, Boeing with its (Apollo-like) CST-100, and Sierra-Nevada Corp's Dream Chaser gliding spaceplane.

Dream Chaser is based on the NASA HL-20 spaceplane.

> It **COST** Canadian **SPACE TOURIST Guy Laliberté $40 MILLION** to **visit** the **ISS** in **2009**.

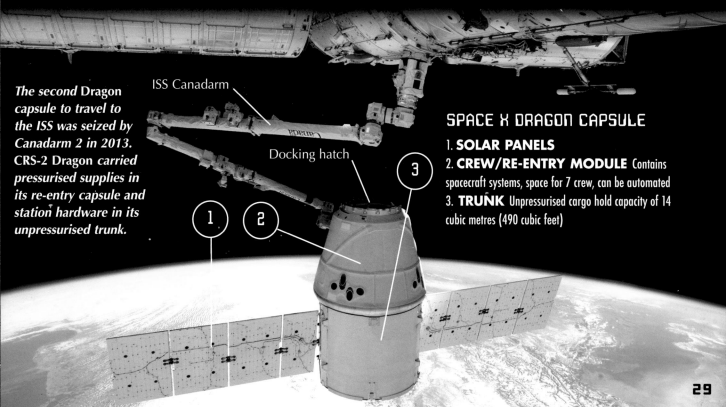

The second Dragon *capsule to travel to the ISS was seized by Canadarm 2 in 2013.* CRS-2 Dragon *carried pressurised supplies in its re-entry capsule and station hardware in its unpressurised trunk.*

ISS Canadarm

Docking hatch

SPACE X DRAGON CAPSULE

1. **SOLAR PANELS**
2. **CREW/RE-ENTRY MODULE** Contains spacecraft systems, space for 7 crew, can be automated
3. **TRUNK** Unpressurised cargo hold capacity of 14 cubic metres (490 cubic feet)

TECH FILES – SPACE FIRSTS

Excludes Apollo Moon missions

FIRST SUB-ORBITAL VEHICLE
V-2 ROCKET DATE: 1944-45 NATIONALITY: German ALTITUDE: 206 km (128 miles) with maximum long-range trajectory NOTES: Ballistic terror weapon

FIRST ORBITAL VEHICLE
SPUTNIK 1 DATE: 4 October 1957 NATIONALITY: Soviet Union ALTITUDE: 215-939 km (134-583 miles) ORBITS: 1,350 NOTES: Experimental satellite

FIRST ANIMAL ORBITAL SPACEFLIGHT
LAIKA DATE: 3 November 1957 NATIONALITY: Soviet Union ALTITUDE: 211-1,659 km (131-1,031 miles) ORBITS: Over 2,000 NOTES: Survived only six orbits

FIRST HUMAN ORBITAL SPACEFLIGHT
YURI GAGARIN DATE: 12 April 1961 NATIONALITY: Soviet Union ALTITUDE: 169-327 km (105-203 miles) ORBITS: One TIME IN SPACE: 1 hour 48 minutes

FIRST SUB-ORBITAL HUMAN SPACEFLIGHT
ALAN SHEPARD DATE: 5 May 1961 NATIONALITY: US ALTITUDE: 187.5 km (101 miles) MISSION DURATION: 15 minutes 22 seconds

FIRST MULTI-CREW SPACEFLIGHT
VOSKHOD 1 DATE: 12 October 1964 NATIONALITY: Soviet Union ALTITUDE: 178-336 km (110-208 miles) ORBITS: 16 CREW: Vladimir Komarov (Commander), Konstantin Feoktistov (Engineer), Boris Yegorov (Doctor) MISSION DURATION: 24 hours 17 minutes

FIRST SPACEWALK
ALEXEY LEONOV DATE: 18 March 1965 NATIONALITY: Soviet Union ALTITUDE: 167-475 km (103-295 miles) EVA DURATION: 12 minutes 9 seconds

FIRST SPACE VEHICLE DOCKING
GEMINI 8 TO AGENA TARGET VEHICLE (ATV) DATE: 16 March 1966 NATIONALITY: US CREW: Neil Armstrong (Commander), David Scott (Pilot) NOTES: Undocked after 31 minutes due to dangerous uncontrolled spinning caused by jammed thrusters on Gemini 8

FIRST MULTI-PERSON SPACEWALK
YEVGENY KHRUNOV & ALEKSEI YELISEYEV DATE: 16 January 1969 NATIONALITY: Soviet Union MISSIONS: Soyuz 4 & 5

FIRST REUSABLE SPACECRAFT
NASA SPACE SHUTTLE INAUGURAL FLIGHT: STS-1, 12 April 1981, Orbiter Columbia FINAL FLIGHT: STS-135, 21 July 2011, Orbiter Atlantis

LONGEST HUMAN SPACEFLIGHT
VALERI POLYAKOV DATE BEGUN: 8 January 1994 NATIONALITY: Soviet Union SPACECRAFT: Mir TIME IN SPACE: 437 days

LONGEST SPACEWALK
JAMES VOSS & SUSAN HELMS DATE: 11 March 2001 NATIONALITY: US MISSION: STS-102 EVA DURATION: 8 hours 56 minutes NOTES: First of two EVAs to prepare a Pressurised Mating Adapter for relocation onboard the International Space Station

FIRST SPACE TOURIST
DENNIS TITO LAUNCH DATE: 28 April 2001 RE-ENTRY DATE: 6 May 2001 NATIONALITY: US SPACECRAFT: ISS TIME IN SPACE: 7 days 22 hours 4 minutes

GLOSSARY

ATMOSPHERE layer of gases around a space object such as a planet

ATTITUDE position of a spacecraft, for example, its angle in relation to Earth, or pointing at a star

ELLIPTICAL oval-shaped, as for the orbits of many planets and spacecraft

ESCAPE VELOCITY speed needed to get away from an object's gravity, like a moon or planet, and become free in space. For Earth it is 11.2 km (7 miles) per second at the surface

EVA Extra Vehicular Activity, being outside a craft in space, often called a spacewalk

GRAVITY force of attraction between objects, which is especially huge for massive objects such as planets and stars

MASS amount of matter in an object, in the form of numbers and kinds of atoms

MICROGRAVITY where the force of gravity from a nearby object, like a planet, is extremely weak or almost zero

MOON space object that orbits a planet. The single moon of Earth is simply known as the Moon (capital letter M)

ORBIT regular path of one object around a larger one, determined by the speed, mass and gravity of the objects

PLANET large space object that has a spherical shape due to its gravity, and has cleared a regular orbital path around a star

RE-ENTRY returning from space to an object such as a planet, when friction with the thickening atmosphere slows the spacecraft but also causes immense heat

RETROROCKETS rockets facing the direction of motion of a craft, fired to slow it down

SATELLITE space object that goes around or orbits another, including natural satellites like the Moon orbiting Earth or Earth orbiting the Sun, and man-made satellites

STAR space object that at some stage is large and dense enough, with enough gravity, to undergo fusion and give out light, heat and similar energy

SUB-ORBITAL a mission that leaves the surface of a planet, flies into space, then comes down again, without going into orbit

INDEX

A
A4 rocket 7
Aldrin, Buzz 16
Apollo program 13, 17, 19, 21
Atlantis orbiter 22, 25
Atlas rocket 14

C
Canadarm 24, 25, 29
Challenger orbiter 22, 24, 26, 27
Columbia orbiter 22, 27
Cooper, Gordon 15, 17

D
Discovery orbiter 22, 25
docking 17, 20, 21
Dream Chaser 29

E
Endeavor orbiter 25
escape velocity 6
Extra Vehicle Activity (EVA) 16, 18

F
Freedom 7 capsule 13
Friendship 7 capsule 14, 15

G
Gagarin, Yuri 10–11
Gemini mission 16–17, 19
Glenn, John 14, 15, 25

Grissom, 'Gus' 14, 17, 19

H
Hand-Held Manoeuvring Unit (HHMU) 19
Hubble Space Telescope 24

I
International Space Station (ISS) 5, 21, 25, 29

J
John F Kennedy Space Center 25
Jupiter rockets 9, 12

K
Kepler, Johannes 4
Korolev, Sergei 8, 10, 20

L
Laika, 8, 9
Leonov, Alexey 18, 19, 21
Lovell, Jim 16, 17

M
Mercury spacecraft 4, 12–15
Mir space station 25

R
R-7 rocket 8, 10, 20
Redstone rocket 9, 12, 13, 14
rendezvous manoeuvre 17

rocket invention 6–7

S
Shepard, Alan 4 13
Shuttle Remote Manipulator System (SRMS) 24
Solid Rocket Boosters 22, 23
Soyuz spacecraft 20–21, 26, 27, 29
Space Shuttles 5, 22–25, 26, 27
space tourism 29
Space Transportation System (STS) 22, 23, 24, 25, 26
Spacelab 24
SpaceShipOne 28
spacewalking 16, 17, 18–19, 24
SpaceX 29
Sputnik 7, 8
Stafford, Thomas 17, 21

T
Tereshkova, Valentina 11
Titan rocket 16
Tsiolkovsky, Konstantin 4, 6

V
V-2 rocket 7
Virgin Galactic 28
von Braun, Wernher 6, 7
Voskhod spacecraft 16, 18
Vostok spacecraft 10, 11, 14